THE OTHER SIDE OF THE ISLAND

The Other Side of the Island

A Collection of Short Stories by

Yvonne Nelson Perry

John Daniel & Co., Publishers

SANTA BARBARA • 1994

"No More Offerings, No More Gifts" was first published in *Tidepools*,
Spring 1991. "The Pig Killer" was first published in *Tidepools*, Spring 1993.
"Variations of Aloha" was first published in *Tidepools*, Spring 1992.
"Canebrake" was first published in *Santa Barbara Review*, Fall 1993.
"White Markers" was first published in *Hawai'i Review*, Spring 1994.
"House of Miseries" was first published in *Hawai'i Review*, Spring 1991.
"Fighting Cocks" was first published in *Hawai'i Review*, Spring 1991.

Design and typography by Jim Cook

Published by John Daniel & Company, a division of Daniel & Daniel,
Publishers, Inc., Post Office Box 21922, Santa Barbara, California 93121

LIBRARY OF CONGRESS CATALOGING-IN-PUBLICATION DATA
    Perry, Yvonne Nelson
        The other side of the island : stories / Yvonne Nelson
    Perry.
        p. cm.
        ISBN 1-880284-06-5
        1. Hawaii—Fiction. I. Title.
    PS3566.E723087 1994
    813'.54—dc20   93-45278
                                                        CIP

For Emma, who taught me how
to tame my unseen dragons.

Ā hui hou kākou, māmā.

Contents

The Other Side of the Island

The Main Event

Twisting and turning, the wounded rooster burrowed into the sawdust. A throng of men surrounding the pit cheered as the victorious fighting cock strutted around the arena.

From the sidelines, Amador watched Tai Sing step into the ring and grab his gamecock. The old man held the winner high. Scanning the audience, Tai Sing's black-beetle eyes found him.

Amador felt his neck hair rise. He looked down at the wire cage beside him. Tonight his rooster would take on its first challenger, a Tai Sing-trained bird.

The cockfighting ring sat in the middle of a huge

tin-roofed shed once used to store pineapple crates and fertilizer. A rangy kamani tree stood beside the squat blockhouse. Hard-packed dirt in front of the abandoned building served as a parking lot; old trucks and new sedans shared the space.

The heavy heat of the day had continued into the evening. Hot as air in a sun-baked metal drum, the temperature inside the shed soared. Perspiration ran into Amador's eyes, the sting of salt bringing tears. He wiped a hand across his forehead, flicking the sweat away.

A pit boss stepped into the center of the gaming arena and held up two hands, fingers spread wide, indicating ten minutes until the next match. He pointed at Amador and Tai Sing, designating the contestants. Alerted by these signals, the noisy "cockers" began to place their bets. Gripping money in tight fists, the men yelled at a half-dozen bookies present, waving bets in their faces. The match between Amador and Tai Sing, both local residents, stimulated heavy wagering.

Amador carried his cage to the edge of the cockpit and squatted beside the holding pen. His soaked tee shirt stuck to his scrawny body, the ribs like fish bones. Slicked-back pomaded hair revealed a tiny gold stud in one ear, a silver coin pressed into the other.

Across the arena, Tai Sing lit a cheroot. Watching him, Amador untied a pouch of tobacco fastened to his belt by the bag's orange drawstring. He extracted a piece of paper tucked inside the sack and rolled a cigarette, sealing it with a lick before lighting it.

A blue haze hung over the crowd, which breathed in the stench of smoke, unwashed bodies and cheap booze. A single bulb hanging in the middle of the vast room swung slowly back and forth, throwing its yellow light across the faces in the crowd. Shadows hid the high cross beams of the shed. In that upper world, fruit rats raced along rotting planks. A foot above the filthy sawdust ring, fat flies hovered, gorged with fresh chicken blood.

The crowd milled about in the carnival atmosphere. The noise increased when the pit boss signaled five minutes until the next contest. A rush of final betting ensued.

Amador stared across the cockpit at Tai Sing. With hooded eyes, the old Chinese man stood wrapped in a black, high-collared robe. A thin hand fondled the red velvet money pouch that hung from his neck by a braided cord. Cobwebs of deep lines covered his gaunt face. Pain from some ancient illness wrinkled his brow; dislike of Amador tightened his lips.

Amador felt Tai Sing's hatred sweep across the pit and enfold him. He had admitted he got the old man's granddaughter pregnant. In love with the girl, he wanted to marry her, but Tai Sing refused to let him see her. The old man made her get an abortion. Amador wondered if Tai Sing felt his hatred, too.

The pit boss signaled for the fighting cocks to enter the ring. All betting ceased as the spectators faced inward.

Amador opened his cage. Slipping one hand beneath his rooster's breastbone, he placed his other hand across its back and gently withdrew the Malay from the enclosure. The wheat-colored sporting chicken had a compact body with long legs, well-muscled and wide-spaced. An irregular strawberry pea comb sat over pearl eyes, short wattles draped over a high chest. Cradling the Malay in his arms, Amador entered the ring with his virgin game bird.

Tai Sing removed his new fighting cock from its wooden cage and stepped over a low board barrier into the pit. Two men followed him. While Amador and Tai Sing held their roosters at arms' length, the attendants attached razor-sharp metal spurs to each fighting cock's ankles.

Calling for the release of the birds, the pit boss clapped his hands together and pointed to spots in front of Amador and Tai Sing.

Tai Sing placed his rooster on the sawdust. With a back shawled in black and green iridescent feathers, the Orloff fowl stood erect and shook itself, ruffling its plumage. Its powerful beak opened and closed, opened and closed. Small wattles and comb offered no points of attack. Extending its thick neck, the Orloff turned its broad head from side to side. Jeweled eyes blinked at the crowd, which rumbled its appreciation of the fine imported bird.

Amador put down his Malay. The gamecock cast a small shadow on the sawdust.

The two men backed out of the ring. The fighting cocks moved forward, strutting and bobbing around each other. Suddenly, the Orloff flapped its wings and leaped into the air, striking the smaller fowl in the side.

The crowd roared.

The Malay responded.

The beating of wings sounded like dry paper crackling. The cocks leaped at each other again and again and again, their double-edged blades ripping and tearing.

The Malay fell beneath the Orloff.

Tai Sing's cock clawed at Amador's rooster until its sharp spurs slit open the Malay's breast. The Malay, half-buried in the blood-wet sawdust, lay still, entrails protruding from its crested chest.

Sour fluid surged up into Amador's mouth. He spit it out. The putrid phlegm left a bitter aftertaste.

Tai Sing stepped into the ring, captured the Orloff, and held the fighting cock high. A tidal wave of noise flooded the shed.

Amador couldn't move.

Glancing over at the young man, Tai Sing moved closer to the disemboweled Malay, placed a shoe on the fallen rooster, and pushed down on the still body. A projectile of blood exploded from the dead gaming bird.

Enraged, Amador leaped into the ring and confronted Tai Sing, who still held his rooster aloft.

"You dog shit!" Amador yelled, shaking a fist in the old man's face. "Stinking dog shit!"

The Orloff reacted, flapping powerful wings tipped with long feelers of black feathers. It spread the darkness wide, freeing itself from Tai Sing's grasp. In flight, the fighting cock slashed at the old man, slicing a deep cut across his neck. Tai Sing clutched his throat with both hands; Amador watched the bright red blood spurt through the old man's fingers as Tai Sing dropped to his knees.

The raucous crowd fell silent. The main event was over.

No More Offerings, No More Gifts

Mrs. Ito heard the clink of ice cubes. She opened her eyes and let her gaze slide over the whiteness of the hospital room.

"Good afternoon," said a young Japanese girl as she filled the water carafe beside Mrs. Ito's bed. "Ready for your outing?"

Mrs. Ito kept her eyes on the edge of nothing as the aide pushed her wheelchair out the door and down the hall.

At the end of the hall, double doors opened onto a ramp that led to the grounds of the Honolulu convalescent home. There the attendant wheeled Mrs. Ito briskly into the shade of a massive banyan tree and left her with a promise to be back soon.

Mrs. Ito sat in the shiny chair, grasping an old cloth purse hidden under the light wrap across her lap. She stared at the exposed roots of the banyan tree as they humped their way across the bare ground.

Both her sons used to play root tag under a banyan in the park near their old home in Kailua. With the other neighborhood children, they had raced along the broad, rough roots with arms outstretched, balancing their wiry bodies, shouting noisily to each other. Sitting there now, she could hear their laughter but she couldn't see them. They darted by so quickly.

Looking around to make sure no one was monitoring her, Mrs. Ito rolled her wheelchair, inch by inch, over the hard-packed dirt toward the bus stop in front of the home. Before she reached the bus stop bench, she pushed her wrap aside, got out of the chair, and shuffled over to the narrow wooden seat. She sat down and settled her bag on her lap; it took only a moment to find her small leather coin purse. Holding carfare tightly in a shriveled hand, she leaned back and wearily closed her eyes.

She saw the airplanes again, with those ominous red circles on the tips of their wings. They came directly at her, but just before they crashed into her, her eyes flew open, wide and terrified. She knew she had to keep her eyes open or the rising suns would explode in her head.

Within moments, a city bus came around the corner and hissed to a stop in front of her. As its door opened, Mrs. Ito gathered her purse and her strength, stood up, and moved toward the bus. Grabbing the handrails, she pulled herself up onto the first step.

"Need some help, obāsan?" asked the driver.

Unassisted, Mrs. Ito mounted the second and last step and stood before the man. She pressed her money into his waiting palm, turned, and sat on the first long seat, near the door.

"Where you want to go, obāsan?" the driver asked.

Mrs. Ito did not answer. She sat hunched over, gripping the slim silver pole at the end of her seat.

"Okay, just let me know when we're there." The driver closed the door, glanced up into his rearview mirror, and pulled away from the curb.

Mrs. Ito looked around at the other passengers. No one looked back at her so she stared at her liver-spotted hands. They were brown, like the uniforms her sons had worn so proudly. She remembered that last day, when their troop ship pulled away from the Honolulu dock. Both boys had waved wildly and shouted the 442nd Regiment's famous motto, "Go for broke!" She stood on the pier and watched her sons fade into the distance; so many went away forever that day.

Mrs. Ito looked out the window; they were almost there. She got up and swayed the few feet to the front of the bus.

19

"Next stop, obāsan?" asked the driver.

Mrs. Ito stood at the top of the steps.

She waited until the bus was out of sight before she turned and started down the lane that led to the Hongwanji Mission. Walking down the deserted road, she finally came to the church's gravel courtyard. She passed through the finely raked area, opened an iron gate, and entered the graveyard beyond.

Moving very slowly now, down the cemetery's main path, Mrs. Ito counted off five rows of tombstones then turned to the right. Five plots over and she was there. Almost every grave in her row had offerings of fruit or flowers; some had brightly wrapped presents.

Mrs. Ito leaned against a gravestone and closed her eyes.

She was on the tramp freighter again, in Hong Kong. She saw the large packing crate fall from the loading crane. It hit the wooden pier and burst open. There was a young Chinese woman inside, with a baby clutched to her bare breast. The Chinese woman was bound for slavery; Mrs. Ito was a Japanese picture bride on her way to Hawaii.

She opened her eyes and sat down on the narrow slab in front of the pillar that bore her husband's name. Unclasping her purse, Mrs. Ito took out a faded photograph of herself wearing a blue kimono with beautiful

white chrysanthemums on it, a silk robe tied with a per-
simmon-colored obi. There was an elegantly styled
hairpiece on her head. She had never before worn such
magnificent clothes, all rented from the marriage broker
in Yokohama. She gazed at the picture for a long time
before slipping it back into her purse.

Now Mrs. Ito took an orange, saved from lunch,
out of her bag and placed it at the base of her husband's
marker.

Standing up, the old woman clasped her frail hands
together and bowed low.

"Thank you, Ito-San. I did not have anything to
lose until you gave me everything."

The Pig Killer

Crouched in a koa-haole thicket, twelve-year-old Annie
Little Lum turned over a flat rock near her bare feet and
watched the sow bugs scatter. She poked a finger at one;
it rolled into a tight ball. Annie picked it up and popped
it into her mouth, swallowing it in a quick gulp. She
wondered if the gray skeleton-like bugs crawled around
in her stomach until they turned blue from lack of
oxygen.

Annie stood and parted the thick tangle of branches
shielding her. She stared at the house in the distance.
Across the back of the sprawling structure hung a huge
sign: *Aloha Luaus,* the vowels in red, the consonants in

yellow. A gigantic wooden flower lei encircled the two words.

Plumeria trees dotted the freshly mowed lawn where row after row of makeshift tables stood, wide boards on squat sawhorses. Tomorrow afternoon they would be covered with ti leaves and hibiscus placed down the middle of each one before the lūʻau guests arrived.

Every Saturday was lūʻau day. Today was Friday, pig-killing day.

For years, Annie Little Lum's mother would take her into a front bedroom of the big house before a pig butchering. Cuddling her, her mother put a pillow over her head when the screeching started. At first, Annie fought against the smothering feel of the soft cushion, but after she heard the pig's high-pitched shrieks, she no longer resisted her mother's attempt to shut out the sounds of the slaughtering.

"Don't make trouble." Every day her mother said the same thing. "If I lose this job, there's no place to go. Please, Annie Little Lum, don't make trouble." Her mother had named her after a grandmother in heaven and a father gone to hell: "Annie, you look a *little* like a Lum."

One day shortly after her fifth birthday, Annie hid in the small shed near the pig-slaughtering yard. Peering through a dirty window facing the killing area, she saw Clegg, the lūʻau boss, and one of the local men who worked for him drag an immense white pig across the lawn. A third man followed carrying a large metal pan.

When the men reached the dirt yard behind the outbuilding, Clegg unsheathed the black-handled knife strapped to his waist. One of the workers straddled the struggling pig and pulled its head up and back. The hog's squeals intensified, rising in volume and pitch.

From her hiding place, Annie watched Clegg step forward. Gripping his butcher knife with both hands, he buried it deep inside the pig's exposed throat and pulled the blade through the soft flesh. The last shriek ended, half-finished.

Annie saw Clegg jump back as a torrent of bright red blood spurted from a long gash in the white neck. The man holding the pan set it under the gushing wound. The other worker shifted his hold on the pig; grabbing the animal by both ears, he held its head over the waiting container. Now the blood ran dark in a wide stream; steam rose from the foaming liquid in the metal basin.

Clegg watched the procedure closely, his face a bleached mask.

Annie didn't see what happened after that. She turned away and threw up everything she had eaten that day. Then the dry heaves began and she vomited yellow bile onto the worn wooden floor of the shed. Exhausted, she huddled on a pile of discarded burlap sacks used to cover the pigs placed in the imu, an underground oven. The bags, stiff and dried out, emitted a musky odor. Annie didn't notice; she fell into a deep, troubled sleep. Her mother found her there later that day.

Now Annie saw her mother come out of the main house and cross to the storage shed. She emerged carrying a bundle of rolled-up lau hala mats; tourists attending the lūʻau sat on them while they ate and watched the hula show. Annie's mother, the lead dancer, did two hula solos during the performance. She called herself Kealoha of Kauaʻi.

Kealoha placed the woven mats on a table and returned to the house.

Beyond the shed, in a remote corner of the grounds, Annie could see the lūʻau workers putting large rocks into the earthen oven. All night a fire inside the pit would heat the smooth lava stones. At dawn tomorrow, the butchered pig, wrapped in burlap bags, would be lowered into the hole. Topped with yams, banana stalks, and more sacks before the final layer of dirt, the main feature of the lūʻau roasted underground until the island visitors assembled for the feast. They came in busloads.

Annie watched the house. Time for the slaughtering. She drew back into the thicket and sat down on the ground cover of damp rotted leaves. Clegg would be coming out soon.

The pig killer lived in the front part of the party house; Annie and her mother shared a room next to the kitchen. Her mother said the new lūʻau manager came from a faraway place called Iowa, from a pig farm on the mainland. Clegg wasn't even hapa haole, half-white, but he'd landed the job because he knew how to butcher pigs and cater banquets and deal with the tourists. They flocked around him during the lūʻau. He wore a tee shirt under his aloha shirt and white buck shoes, like the haole men. He could speak their language, especially the haole women's, her mother said.

While Clegg postured his way through the evening, Annie's mother and the dance troupe, the hālau, served the kālua pig and did hula after hula until the buses hauled the sated crowd back to their Waikiki hotels.

This afternoon the rain clouds circled in, hugging the steep slope of the range behind the house. A sudden shower washed the surrounding tropical plants, leaving them shiny and metallic-looking. The rain stopped as abruptly as it started.

Kealoha came out of the house and crossed to the shed. She went in, leaving the door ajar.

Clegg, butcher knife belted in place, strode across the lawn a moment later, entered the tin-roofed building, and closed the door behind him.

Annie Little Lum pushed aside the koa branches and stepped out of the thicket. Skirting the tables, she darted across the wet grass. Staying close to one side of the shed, she inched her way around a corner until she stood directly under the window facing the slaughtering area.

She heard her mother's voice.

"No. You have no right," said Kealoha.

"Shut up, woman, you don't have any rights."

Annie heard metal cans clattering to the plank floor.

"Stop it, Clegg! You're hurting me."

"You'll feel good in a minute. You always do."

More noise: tiki torches clanking against each other. Her mother's voice again, begging.

"Clegg, stop. Please."

Then the sound of slaps and a cry. It was low-pitched and falling.

Annie slumped to the ground. She bit down hard on her lower lip, and stared at the dark stain where last week's bleeding had missed the pan. She closed her eyes; from the river in her mind, a pig with a slit throat appeared. She covered her ears with her hands, but the screaming continued from within.

Scrambling to her feet, Annie ran across the clearing to the pig sty in a ravine at the bottom of the property. She unhooked the wire loop that secured the pen's slat gate. Swinging it open, she faced the motionless animal inside. The young sow stared back at her with flat black eyes.

"Run, you stupid pig. Run!"

She stepped around the animal and, bracing herself

against the fence of the small enclosure, placed one foot on its rump and pushed.

"Move! Get out of here!"

The pig took two steps and stopped.

Annie tried again, kicking at the sow's hindquarters.

"Out! Hayaku! Go!"

This time the pig moved. Snorting, it struggled up the slight incline to the main yard and trotted toward the shed.

"No!" Annie screamed, chasing it. "No!"

She tried to head off the pig, waving her hands and jumping in front of the lumbering animal. They reached the lean-to; Clegg opened the door and stepped outside. Both Annie and the pig stopped.

"Well, well, well. Annie Little Lum is our new pig driver. Bringing her in for the kill, girl?"

Annie looked past Clegg. Her mother stood in the doorway, clutching the front of her shirt. Kealoha bowed her head and looked down at her bare feet.

Annie glanced from her mother to Clegg, then turned and raced for her secret spot. Hidden within the tangled mass of branches swollen with bean pods, she watched Clegg herd the loose sow toward the back of the shed. A yell for his helpers brought them running. One held the large metal pan.

Hunkered deep in the undergrowth, Annie Little Lum saw the men enter the slaughtering yard. At her feet, a gray bug searched for a hiding place. Annie bent over and picked up the insect. It tightened into a tiny ball; she let it roll off her palm, open up, and crawl away.

Variations of Aloha

The woman and the horse walked shoulder to shoulder through the honohono grass of the high pasture. Behind them loomed Maui's extinct volcano, its towering peak covered by clouds. Far below, the town of Pā'ia nestled in a giant stand of eucalyptus trees. Beyond lay a horizon of blue water.

It grew lighter as they headed makai, toward the sea, still miles away. The young woman remembered the times they'd ridden this trail to the ocean, to canter on the hot sand, then splash through the cool surf.

Lost in her memories, she didn't notice the horse's limp. It was only when his lead rope caught on a kukui

tree branch and she stopped to release it that she saw him hesitate, then stumble as they started up again.

"Not going to make it to the beach, are you?"

The woman patted the gelding's forehead and ran a hand down his roached mane.

"That's okay, old man. We'll go to the other place now."

She turned the horse and started off in a new direction. The going was rougher now because these paths were seldom used. Once, a lone mongoose appeared on the trail ahead of them; it froze, then darted into a orange tumble of lantana.

Finally they broke out of the tangle of wild pasture grasses and shrubs onto a vast pineapple field. Slowly, the woman maneuvered the horse between two rows of the stiff-leaved plants.

The sun had come up over Haleakalā, the House of the Sun mountain, and the air began to lose its morning crispness. Beads of perspiration formed across the woman's nose. She put a hand on the horse's bony withers to see if he felt sweaty. At her touch, he stopped.

"You all right?"

She stood beside the horse, rubbing his soft muzzle.

"It's not far now," she told him.

She made a kissing sound and moved on.

The horse needed no further urging. Together, they continued until they came to a deep ditch on the far side of the field.

"Come on, old man. Follow me."

The woman started down the steep incline. Stepping ahead and to one side of him, she tugged on the lead line. The horse followed her willingly, slipping and sliding down to the bottom. There she coaxed him into the shade of the squat guava trees growing in the ravine. Two displaced mynah birds shrieked their disapproval and took flight.

Pulling down hard on the rope, the woman commanded the old sorrel to kneel, a trick she had used when she was small and couldn't reach the stirrups. The horse had learned to go down on his knees and wait until she was safely in the saddle before rising. This time, his forelegs buckled; his entire body ended up on the ground. To keep him there, the woman stroked his neck.

"Just lie still," she said. "We're not going anywhere."

Convinced he was down to stay, she took off her palaka and brushed them off as best she could, streaking the blue-and-white shirt with the dust and dirt of the long walk. Finishing the chore, she put her shirt back on and sat cross-legged beside the horse.

Now she reached into a back pocket of her frayed jeans and took out a narrow box. Opening it, she removed a syringe and a bottle of cloudy liquid.

"We have to do this together, old man," she told the horse. He whinnied as he nuzzled her shoulder.

Suddenly the woman thrust the needle and the vial back into the box and threw it to the ground. She cupped both hands over her mouth to keep from crying aloud.

The horse nuzzled her again.

She lowered her hands and spoke quietly to him.

"Please understand. I can't let anyone else do this."

Putting her sun-dark arms around his thin neck, she laid her head against his; he smelled like pineapple bran, sweet and musty.

Then the woman wept for them both.

When silence floated across the field once more, she picked up the box lying in the dirt.

For a long time the woman sat with the horse's head cradled in her lap. When the sun was over West Maui, she got up, climbed the steep bank, and began to push the soft, warm Hawaiian soil over the horse at the bottom of the ditch.

Home on the Blue

It started out as an ordinary charter.

At daybreak, four tourists from the mainland boarded my marlin fishing boat, the *Pua Kai*. With my oldest son, Pekelo, at the helm, we slipped out of Honokōhau, a docking inlet blasted out of an ancient lava flow ten miles from Kailua-Kona. Night lights behind us on the slopes of Mauna Kea faded in the early morning sun. The open sea, a liquid mirror, stretched before us.

As we headed north, Kekauliki, my deck hand for over twenty years, set up the outrigger lines. Terrified of sharks, the huge full-blooded Hawaiian claims the manō as his ʻaumakua, his personal god. The way he figures, if he ever falls overboard in shark-infested waters, he'll be family, not food.

We caught kawakawa, Pacific bonito, to use as live bait, then spent the morning trolling rigs in a zig-zag pattern. A mile off the Kona Gold Coast, the ocean is six hundred fathoms. That's where the blue marlin roam.

After an ʻono lunch of ham sandwiches and Primo beer, the big-game sportsfishers retreated to various areas of the fifty-five-foot power boat to relax. The fourth man, a skinny haole from New York City, sat strapped in the fishing chair on the stern. Trolling behind the transom, his bait ran clear of the prop wash.

From the flying bridge, I watched the kawakawa skim through the clear water. A shadow appeared about twenty feet behind the live bait, stalking it. Suddenly, an iridescent flash cut through the water. A blue had shown his colors.

The New Yorker's reel screamed.

"Marlin!" I yelled.

Bounding down the ladder to the main deck, I checked the chair harness to make sure the Big Apple Man had been securely buckled in. I concentrated on his reel. With a forty-five-pound drag, its spinning speed told me the guy had hooked a big one. Maybe even a grander, a thousand-pounder. Billfish that size are taken in Hawaiian waters but not as often as they're caught off Australia.

"Strike him!" I shouted. "Set the hook!"

The man in the chair froze, clearly unable to jerk the line taut.

At the wheel, Pekelo waited for my signal. I waited for the New Yorker to set his hook.

The man didn't move.

I looked up at my son and pointed forward. Pekelo gunned the engines, enough to bury the hook deep, then throttled down. The marlin felt the steel and made a full-power run away from the *Pua Kai*.

Now the man in the chair reacted; he started to work the rod.

The battle had begun.

The a'u, a marlin the size of a small horse, sounded and soared, raced and ran. Time after time, it heaved its bulk skyward and danced across the top of the water, slashing its bill from side to side.

For the first hour, the man in the fishing chair kept the line moving. As the marlin took it out, the man brought it back in. When the fisherman tired, the marlin used his massive weight to keep the line taut while its muscles recovered.

For an IGFA record, I couldn't help the tourist land his fish, merely talk him through the ordeal.

"Keep pumping the rod," I told the exhausted man. He kept trying to winch the line in. "Pump! Reel in on the downward pump."

The sun beat down on the poor guy, frying any

exposed white skin. He looked like an 'ōpae-'ula, a red shrimp. I gave him a swig of cold beer, and poured the rest over his head.

After two grueling hours, the marlin gave up the fight and let itself be reeled in.

With Pekelo topside at the wheel, Kekauliki and I positioned ourselves to gaff the billfish. At the stern, I reached for the leader. With gloved hands, I grabbed the thin cable and, hand-over-hand, pulled the marlin close to the boat. Kekauliki stood beside me, ready to gaff the big blue.

Suddenly the marlin rolled and pushed off the *Pua Kai.* The movement twisted the leader around my forearm, jerking me off the boat. The tangled line tightened. The revived fish took off with me strapped to its back.

Auwē, I thought, I'm riding a marlin!

As the billfish leaped over the flat sea, I could barely breathe. Water rushed into my mouth and up my nose. The churning foam blinded me. I knew I couldn't free myself; the cable had pinned me to the marlin.

"Pekelo!" my mind screamed. "Reverse the engines!" The billfish would sound if it felt any tension. I didn't know it at the time but my son immediately punched the boat into reverse, giving the marlin some slack.

One of the tourists on board told me later the New Yorker in the chair kept yelling, "Cut the line! Cut the line!" Kekauliki said he yanked the rod out of the man's hands, then shouted to the others to clear the swivel fighting chair and buckle him in. "Hell with the hands-off rule," Kekauliki told them. "That's my skipper out there. I'm getting him back."

Out on the blue, I cowboyed the scaly bronc first in one direction, then in another. My arm felt as if it had been cut to the bone. Thousands of water needles stabbed my eyes. My body felt as if it had been split open, letting the saltwater rush through.

In bits and pieces, my whole life flashed through my mind. A picture of my four sons popped into my head. Through the roar of the water, I heard unexplainable, low-pitched sounds, like voices. I'm drowning, I thought. The marlin I've killed all my life is now killing me.

Pekelo said he maneuvered the boat as Kekauliki played that fish out and back, out and back. In twenty minutes, the old Hawaiian landed it. I mean us. He and the other fishermen pulled the billfish alongside, using two gaffs and a killing hammer on it.

I couldn't open my eyes until they cut me off the marlin's blue-gray back, hauled me aboard, and laid me on the deck. Blood oozed from the hundreds of slashes made by the billfish's razor-sharp scales. My released arm, limp at my side, throbbed. I raised my head and looked down at my raw body. The force of the rushing water had stripped off my favorite swim trunks.

Kekauliki gave me a hug and a toothless grin. He

even kissed me, though he denies it to this day. He's a
great fisherman; I'm living proof.

My son and Kekauliki secured the giant marlin
across the swim step on the stern. By its girth, they fig-
ured it weighed about nine hundred pounds. No
grander. I probably wore a hundred pounds off it during that wild ride.

As we turned and headed back, Pekelo radioed in,
giving the dockmaster the highlights of our fishing trip.
Townspeople, more tourists, and an ambulance greeted
us at the main pier in Kailua-Kona. Tying up, I heard
Kekauliki yell to the crowd, "The marlin no eat
Captain Rope! Only take him for one ride."

Except for a dislocated shoulder and a year of
bloodshot eyes, only tiny white scars remain all over
my body.

I've never heard of anyone else riding a marlin, or
living to tell the story if they did. Hell, I don't think
about that ride as much as I think about that skinny
haole from New York City who picked up his movie
camera and recorded the whole thing. He sold it to a
television sports program.

That guy got the bucks, but I got the thrills and the
name: The Marlin Riding Man. A marlin riding man
who realizes that the most important thing, when you
leave a harbor, is getting back.

Canebrake

The mongoose came in the middle of the night. Standing by the kitchen window, watching for Joaquin, Kala saw its shadow slink down the path leading to the chicken house. Moments later she heard the squawking and wing-flapping of their lone hen. Grabbing the flashlight from the counter, Kala banged out the screen door and ran down the walk to the hen house.

The beam of light caught the mongoose inside the small chicken yard. The sleek animal froze in its tracks and turned its head toward the light, teeth bared, eyes of black coral ringed in smoky gray. Its stiff brown body hair stood erect.

Kala shouted, and the mongoose darted under the chicken wire fence and fled across the back yard. It disappeared into a tangle of weeds at the edge of the canebrake behind the house.

Inside the coop, Kala found an egg, its shell broken, its insides sucked dry. The hen clucked in a corner, feathers ruffled but unharmed.

She went back to the house to bed, but she couldn't sleep.

Shortly before dawn, Joaquin slipped through the unhooked kitchen screen door. Kala remained motionless when her husband slid under the covers beside her. The ancient koa bedstead creaked as he rolled onto his side, his back toward her.

When he had settled himself, Kala inched closer to him. Putting an arm over his hunched shoulder, she whispered in his ear. "Where have you been, Joaquin? I waited up for you again."

He sighed, feigning sleep, but she could feel his heart pounding. The musky odor of crushed gardenias clung to his warm body. Kala moved back to her side of the bed, away from the scent.

The next morning, after Joaquin left for work, driving an island tour bus, Kala tried to fix the chicken wire fencing around the hen house. A mean structure, the coop afforded no protection against the marauding mongoose.

With razor-sharp claws, it continued to dig shallow

tunnels under the wire mesh, invade the chicken house, and steal the solitary hen's daily egg. Kala found loose boards behind their dilapidated shed and drove them deep into the last hole the mongoose had made; she had refilled the holes with dirt, but that did not keep the animal out. Stopping once for lunch, by late afternoon she had reinforced the entire enclosure with scraps of wood.

He isn't going to stop.

She stared at the speckled hen; it had laid an egg and stood preening itself in the late afternoon sun. Shooing it into the hen house, she took the fresh egg and went indoors.

At sunset she made herself a second banana sandwich, wrapping the fresh bread around the soft peeled fruit. She ate it outside, on the back porch, watching the chicken yard.

After dark the trade winds stopped singing through the cane fields; the choir of green stalks rustled into silence.

Joaquin's late again.

Kala entered the house and lay down on the pūneʻe in the living room. She often slept on the bed-like sofa. Once, half-asleep, she thought she heard the hen flap its wings but it was only a pueo. The owl beat its way low over the cane, a dull thrumming sound echoing into the night.

The full moon came up and passed its midnight position but still the mongoose kept its distance.

Kala dozed.

Startled awake by a loud squawk, she jumped up and raced through the kitchen, grabbing the flashlight on her way. Halfway down the footpath, the squawking stopped.

Outside the chicken yard she flashed a beam of light along the bottom of the mesh fence. The mongoose had dug a new tunnel.

With a shaky hand, Kala twisted the stick of wood that held the chicken yard gate closed and entered the coop. Hearing the thrashing of wings, she shone the light inside the hen house. The multi-colored fowl twitched in a pool of blood, its head nearly severed. With no egg to steal, the mongoose had attacked the chicken. Then, scared away by her noisy approach, it hadn't had time to finish the kill.

Kala turned and leaned against the outside of the hen house. She heard the chicken flop across the rough boards inside; it lodged in a corner and thumped rhythmically against the wall, the sound like a heartbeat. Soon, only the faint scratching noise of its claws could be heard.

Where was Joaquin?

She had been holding her breath. Now she took in great gulps of air. The mongoose would be back, to feed upon the hen.

She ran back to the isolated house surrounded by cane fields. Inside, she went directly to the narrow hall closet and took out Joaquin's rifle. By the flashlight's glow, she loaded the .22 from a box on the closet shelf.

On the kitchen stoop, Kala sat on the top step and hugged the gun to her breasts. The humid air wrapped the world around her in a shroud, the silence broken only by a rare nighttime fluttering of cane tassels. Keeping her eyes on the coop, she waited.

When the early morning light touched the darkest shadows and the wind shook the sleeping cane awake, Kala heard the whine of their pickup.

She placed the gun gently across her knees.

Joaquin pulled into the back yard and parked behind the hen house. Through the chicken wire fence, Kala saw him sit up straight and check his face in the rearview mirror. He wore the red hibiscus aloha shirt she'd given him for his last birthday; he wiped his mouth across one sleeve.

Easing the door open, then shut, Joaquin got out of the truck and walked around the corner of the chicken coop. Running his hands over his stiff rumpled hair, he headed for the kitchen door.

Kala raised the rifle butt to her shoulder. The mongoose was back.

White Markers

Jiro Haneda went fishing on what should have been his wedding day. The long-awaited Shinto ceremony had been canceled. Mitsumi, his bride, was gone. She had left him a note.

Jiro, I can not marry you.

He drove his jeep to Makapuʻu and parked in the lot overlooking the point. All along the rugged shoreline, he could see slender pillars marking places where careless fishermen had been washed off rock ledges into the turbulent sea.

Staring at the closest four-foot concrete post, Jiro slipped off his thongs and pulled on a pair of black tabi.

The canvas-like anklet socks had rubber soles for gripping power and protection against ʻaʻā, rough lava.

He walked to the rear of the jeep. The salt air of the islands had rusted out sections of its side panels, leaving a filigree of olive-green metal. He ran his fingers across the frail network.

Jiro, I can not marry you.

A fishing pole protruded from the back of the topless vehicle. Jiro eased the rod out and removed the scrap of faded red bandanna tied to the tapered end. Reaching into the recess behind the driver's seat, he picked up his battered tackle box full of bait and hand-tied lures.

Keeping his legs far apart for balance, Jiro maneuvered down the rocky incline that led to the fishing ledge below. Closer to the surf pounding against the massive cliff, the noise swelled. The dry rocks turned black, wet with spray. Tiny translucent crabs poised on the slick surfaces darted into invisible crevices.

Jiro stopped and shifted the tackle box to his hand holding the pole. He looked over at Rabbit Island, a barren rock formation offshore. Midafternoon, there were purple shadows on its leeward side. Riptides around the miniature islet kept it free of invading explorers.

He glanced up at the sun, afire in the cloudless sky. The blazing eyeball of the world glared back at him.

Jiro, I can not marry you.

He continued his descent in a crouched position, using his free hand to steady himself on the closest boulder. Gusty winds blew ocean spray high above, speckling the sky with flecks of foam. Slowly, he approached the concrete pillar.

On the ledge, a carpet of water bubbled at his feet. Jiro squatted, placed the tackle box on a nearby rock, and opened it with one hand. He removed a chunk of squid; the stench of the bait mixed with the salty air. With his rod in the crook of an arm, he baited the hook with practiced hands. Tying a light casting weight to the line, he snapped the box shut and stood.

Raising both arms to one side, Jiro whipped the pole back, then thrust it forward. The line zinged out and down, clearing the tumble of rocks beneath him.

He moved toward the white marker.

Jiro, I can not marry you.

The first wave took him by surprise, coming up from under the outcropping. It climbed high, directly in front of him, blocking his view of the open sea. The gigantic waves, in sets of seven, had begun. Startled, he stepped back, jerking his pole upward as the wave rolled over him.

I have deceived you.

Legs awash in water, he felt a pull on the line. His arm muscles knotted in response. With one hand on the reel, he fought back against the tugging. Bracing his legs, he inched forward, playing out the line.

51

A second wave hit, cascading over him. His hunched body cut a path through the curtain of water.

I have loved someone else for a long, long time.

A third wave.

But he is already married and will not leave his wife.

The fishing rod flew out of his hands. Connected to the sea, the pole disappeared over the brim of the rocky crag.

The next wave, bigger than the last, staggered him. Its backflow lashed at his legs, pushing him closer to the edge.

I am carrying his child.

Another wave smashed into him, forcing him to his knees. Jiro took the brutal slamming on his shoulders and back. He watched the water swirl around him. With head bowed, he waited for the next attack.

I can not live with the shame I have brought upon you and my family.

The sixth wave burst out of the ocean like an explosion. It knocked him face down on the razor-sharp rocks; blood gushed from deep slashes on his chin. The saltwater raked through his nostrils like dry sand. Choking, Jiro twisted onto his back, arms spread-eagled.

And the child must not suffer this humiliation.

The final wave rose from the depths of the raging sea. A solid wall of water, it crested over him, hanging there like a white-maned monster. With a thundering roar, it crashed down on him.

Goodbye, Jiro.

The body of water engulfed him. It surged around him, sucking at him, pulling on him. Dragging him toward the sea, it washed him against the white marker.

For a moment Jiro clung to it.

Forgive me.

Then he released his hold on the concrete post.

The receding wave swept over the pillar, rushed to the edge of the jagged cliff, and delivered Jiro to the waiting sea.

Mitsumi

All the Mornings of My Life

I slide a hand down over my belly and find the flat place where, a lifetime ago, a baby had been. I remember the quickening of my body, the heaviness of the child within; I wanted to turn inside-out and nuzzle it. Now I bring out the secret locked in my heart: when the baby was born, I gave him away, a tiny precious gift, never to be returned.

I turn onto my side and see the early morning moon dip low and spill moonbeams over the garden outside my bedroom window. A banyan tree casts spidery shadows on my bed. I grip the cool sheets, pull them over my timeworn body and try to remember a shard of my dream. Maybe there's something in it that's real, something in it I can keep. I shift under the covers and the dream drifts away.

Huddled in my quietness, I try to recall yesterday, any yesterday, any trail I've left behind. I constantly stalk my life, lost in the tangled paths of my mind. Senile dementia, the clinic doctor calls it.

My short-term memory is gone but I still remember, vividly, certain things in the distant past: hands ripping off my clothes, eyes with pupils of black zeros, a small warm baby.

Over the years the image of my son, once clear as a portrait, has faded, blurred, run itself together into a sea of faces I've seen all my life. Now my child is not only lost, he is faceless.

I uncurl myself from the warm haven of my bed and pad to the sliding screen door that opens onto a meandering tropical garden, shared by everyone in the senior citizen compound. I lose my way in my life; I keep a map of the garden on my desk. The drawing leads me through the lush growth of ti leaves, hibiscus, and birds of paradise. Sometimes the gravel paths, lined with thickets of apple-green fern, and the miniature wooden bridges over mounds of earth with topknots of stiff Japanese grass, are walkways into my past, when I was young and making memories.

Standing in the doorway, clutching my thin nightgown around me, I stare at the lofty palms, their raised spiked arms outlined in the morning light. Someone must have picked a lehua blossom; the picking brings a crystal mist down over the garden. The fragrance from the wet ginger is overpowering.

I think I'm getting better when all the time I'm getting worse. I devour the newspaper each morning, but by late afternoon I forget what the world is doing. I write notes to myself and label everything, then worry I'll forget how to read. Every day now, I go over a copy of the letter I sent to the adoption agency so many, many years ago: *If my son ever comes looking for me, please tell him where I am.*

My life is being stripped away, layer by layer. I'm aware of the changes now, but will I know when they've become advanced? Soon, only the first memories will be left. When the memory of my son is gone, how will I know him when he comes? I have this feeling he's about to appear, and I'm about to disappear.

Daylight is hiding in the leafy shadows of the garden now, waiting for its time. Noisy mynahs assemble under the kukui trees, holding a daybreak court.

Sometimes I don't know who I am when I wake. I read old letters and pore through family photo albums daily, trying to make all the pieces fit. A family is a long chain of people. Someone holds onto you, you hold onto someone, and that person holds on to someone else. If everyone holds on tight, you always know who you are. All the links in my family are broken, and I don't have pictures of my son.

I remember staring through schoolyard fences, at little children playing. I'd pick out one child and pretend he belonged to me. One day, I became hysterical when my make-believe child fell off the swings and skinned his knees.

For years I haunted shopping centers and city parks, looking for my son. I thought, I'll know him when I see him; I'm looking for him through a mother's eyes. Once, in a half-dream, I saw him run across my closed eyelids. I squeezed them together, tighter, but he never came back. Now he's like the daylight, waiting in the shadows.

The tent of darkness in the garden rises. Ghosts of clouds float into the valley and a warm rain begins to fall. The garden sentinel, a lone peacock, shrieks. The off-key outbursts hang for long melancholy moments in the heavy tropical air.

Voiceless, in my heart, I call to my son.

As I return to the refuge of my bed, I hear the rustling bamboo whisper, "Why do you cry?"

Someone outside the garden gate clatters by on wooden geta, the elevated slippers splashing through gathering pools of water.

I pull my last memories over me, like a blanket, to cover my loneliness and despair. Slipping a hand over my belly again, I chant my morning prayer: come find me, child, before it's too late, come find me, child, before it's too late.

After Birth

Abraham watched the sharks circle the laboring whale. He had witnessed a courtship here, now he was witnessing a killing.

A year ago, he dove for squid in this inlet on the windward side of the island. Shortly before sunrise, he had slipped overboard into the warm water, making ever-expanding ripples in the glassy surface. Before he reached the cooler depths, he heard voice-like squeals and shrieks. The sounds filtered through the green water, reverberating around him.

The voices stopped.

Abraham sensed something about to happen, like

being on a wild pig hunt when the birds stop singing, moments before a roused boar charges.

Now the sea was silent.

Two humpback whales came into view. Abraham had no place to hide, nowhere to go. His outrigger had drifted too far away. He surfaced, gulped some air and sank back underwater a few feet. He watched the humpbacks approach.

Moving their flukes slowly up and down, the whales glided silently by, as in a dream. They slid through the sea stroking each other's sides with their fins. Then the male shifted his great weight until he was under the female. His thick muscular penis emerged, pale pink in the murky light. It swayed, snaked, then entered the female's genital slit. Belly to belly, flippers wrapped around each other, the whales moved forward, undulating, arching upward and backward in a graceful dance. Suddenly their bodies convulsed and they moved apart, the male running his fluke slowly over the female. Their mating finished, the gentle giants swam away, side by side.

Abraham kicked his way to the surface, gasping for breath. He headed for his outrigger, bobbing low in the water a short distance away. After he climbed into the ancient wooden boat, he pulled off his face mask and sat with head bowed, shaken by what he had seen.

He remembered thinking about Girlie then. He thought about her now.

Girlie. Sweet, motherless Girlie. His child. Eighteen years of dark eyes, tangled nut-brown hair, and secret smiles. One day she wanted to be a movie star and minced about in her faded bathing suit and a tiara woven out of stiff strands from the hala tree in their back yard; the next day, as Queen Emma, she paraded down the beach with a cape of seaweed trailing from her shoulders.

Abraham focused on the scene in front of him. The female humpback lay on the surface, belly up. She arched her knobbed head back, straining in prolonged labor. The sharks circled, patiently awaiting the birth.

Mesmerized by the whale and the sharks, Abraham leaned over the side of the boat, palmed some water, and splashed it on his face and bare chest. Shivering in the heat of the sun, his thoughts returned to Girlie.

When she ran wild, teasing the boys around the fishing dock, he scolded her harshly. One day he slapped her across the face. She ran from him and hid under the pier until he found her there, before dawn. Everyone in town told him Girlie would settle down, but that didn't happen in time; she ran away with a boy from the other side of the island. Abraham didn't even know his name. He didn't go after her. He didn't want her back, not then. Months later, she sent word across the island that she needed him. He went to her but it was too late. His Girlie, Abigail Mahele Kalama, died that day, as the sun went down. He brought home his baby granddaughter; she reminded him of the child he had lost.

Now he watched the sharks tighten their circle.

The humpback, her barnacle-scarred body heaving, rolled from side to side, churning the water. Then she shuddered violently and a cloud of blood appeared around her fluke. The exhausted mother whirled onto her belly, severing the umbilical cord, and the newborn calf fell free, tail-first into the deep.

The sea behind Abraham broke in two. Startled, he jumped to his feet and spun around, nearly capsizing his boat. He saw another humpback whale falling backward into the water after a mighty leap into the air. Within seconds, the gigantic mammal breached again. With half of its body out of the water, it raised its flippers and swung them behind its back. There was a loud *kawoosh* sound as the whale hit the water. Abraham realized that a helpmate female whale, called an auntie, had arrived. She swam under the sinking newborn and nosed it to the surface for its first breath of air.

The sharks stopped circling. Ignoring the baby and the new arrival, they attacked the mother whale. Drained of her strength, she floated, motionless, huge tongue extended. One by one, the three sharks streaked in and slashed at the exposed tongue, ripping off large chunks of purple flesh.

Frantic, Abraham knelt in the outrigger and beat the water with a paddle. The frenzied running attacks continued.

The mother's tongue hung from her mouth in

shreds, the water around it awash with blood. The next target, her soft underbelly.

Abraham knew he couldn't help the mother; he heard her moaning her last whale's song. He searched the surrounding area for her offspring.

The auntie whale, abeam of him in a vertical position with her head above water, looked directly at him. Spy-hopping, she turned her head in the direction of the slaughtering, then submerged and nudged the newborn toward the open sea.

A shark veered away from the killing scene and headed toward the retreating whales.

"No! No!" Abraham stood up and shouted. "Dear God, not the baby, too!"

Beyond the shark, a long line of spray appeared across the surface of the water. A school of spinner dolphins approached at breakneck speed and headed straight for the sharks. A dozen or more, they quickly corralled all three of the sharks into the narrow end of the inlet, close to the rough rocks. With high-pitched shrieks, the dolphins took turns racing in and smashing the sharks into the jagged lava. They crashed head-first into the killers until the sharks' bodies were pulpy hulks in a sea of blood.

Still excited, the dolphins sped to the sea-face of the bay. At the mouth of the secluded cove, they leaped high into the air, one by one, spinning as they fell back into the blue sea.

Hunched in his boat, Abraham shielded his eyes against the glare of the sun and peered at the horizon. In the distance, the guardian whale spouted, sending up a plume of white water. He spotted the calf by its side.

Picking up an oar, Abraham paddled to the mother whale's side. Placing a hand against the mutilated body, he drifted with the still, dark mass until it slipped beneath the smooth surface. Then he turned his outrigger toward shore and home. Girlie's baby needed him.

The Five-Dollar Dive

They brought the guy out at four Saturday afternoon.

They had him on a stretcher, wrapped in a gray blanket. It must have been a job, bringing him down that rough trail from the falls. The men carrying him were dripping in sweat.

As I stood by the ambulance, watching them load up, Jojo appeared at my side.

"A tourist," he snickered. "Shoulda stayed in Waikiki."

Pock-faced Jojo, only fourteen, but already bigger than my father, a stevedore on the Honolulu docks.

Everyone says Jojo is slow, you know, in the head,

but he manages to get money and school lunches away from the rest of us kids.

That's why I'm here. Jojo bet me I couldn't dive off the top of the falls.

Diving at the falls is dangerous. If you don't know what you're doing, you get hurt. Like that tourist. You see, there's this big rock that juts up from the pool's bottom. It's right where you land when you dive off the different ledges. If you go off the lower ones, no problem. You don't go under that deep. You dive off the higher ones, you better know exactly where that underwater rock is or you'll hit it head-on.

Checking out the rock's position is tricky. The water in the pool is dark unless the sun's shining on it. Even then, you can barely see the shadow of that monster under there. Sometimes when I dive, I have to shift back and forth, back and forth, squinting, until I see it.

Anyway, today is the day. Dive off the top of the falls or give Jojo five bucks. You don't tell Jojo what the bet is, he tells you. Remember, he's bigger than the rest of us, and you never know what he's going to do. One day, Benny Sato wouldn't give Jojo his sushi, so Jojo picked him up and threw him over the schoolyard fence. Benny broke his arm when he landed on it wrong; he told the school nurse he was goofing around and fell.

Now, Jojo grabbed my shoulder and pushed me toward the trail that led to the falls.

"Come on, Packy. Dive time," he said.

"Maybe the falls are closed, Jojo. You know, because of that guy." I jerked my thumb toward the ambulance easing out of the dirt parking lot, no siren necessary.

"What's the matta', kid? You afraid?"

To show him I wasn't, I raced for the trail. At that moment I wasn't afraid of diving, I was afraid of Jojo.

The trail rises gradually as it winds through the narrow valley, thick with ginger and ti. Breadfruit trees crowd out the sky, making the trail dark. It always smells like rotten guavas and something else. The guys pee in the bamboo clumps along the way; I guess the girls do it in the pool.

We pounded up the half-mile trail; I could hear Jojo behind me, grunting as he ran flat-footed over the muddy footpath.

As we rounded the last bend, I heard the roar of the waterfall. When I broke out into the open area near the pool, some of the kids from school were in the water. Others were sitting around, strumming ukes, kicking back.

"Hey, Packy! You see the guy?"

"Man, you shoulda been here."

They crowded around, all giving details of the diving accident at once.

Jojo appeared a few moments later. Everyone fell silent; they must have remembered the bet. Only Jojo's sister, Kalei, sunning with the older girls, called to him.

"Show 'em how, Jojo!" she said. She stood on the far bank, wet white tee shirt clinging to her nut-brown body.

Older than her brother, Kalei couldn't wait for Jojo to play football so she could fool around with the team. The football coach wanted Jojo this year, but Mr. Price, our principal, said eighth-grade boys couldn't play. The other teams were glad; bad enough he was going to start next year.

As Jojo strutted over to me, I looked up at the falls. Water tumbled down fifty-five feet, making a foamy circle where it hit the pool. The white water calmed down quickly, however, as the circle widened. When it reached the edges of the pool, it lapped softly against smooth mossy rocks.

"Let's go, Pack Rat."

Jojo elbowed me and pointed to the top ledge.

Nodding, I took off my shirt, tossed it aside, and dove in. I swam across the pool to the rocks beside the falls, pulled myself out of the water, and started to scale the lava cliff.

Jojo was right behind me.

Looking for handholds and crevices for my feet took all my attention. The falls cascaded a few feet away, spraying me with a fine cool mist. Stopping to rest, I glanced down and saw everyone looking up at us. I couldn't hear them, I only saw their mouths open and shut, open and shut.

Jojo grabbed one of my ankles.

"Chickenin' out?" he shouted up at me.

I jerked my foot away in answer and started climbing again.

A few more feet and I scrambled onto the topmost ledge. I had never been this high before. I didn't stand up until Jojo was beside me; we stood up together.

Without a word, we squared off and jung-keenapo'ed to see who would dive first. I threw paper: hand open, fingers spread wide. On the same downstroke, Jojo held out two fingers: scissors to cut my paper.

I had to dive first.

I turned and faced the pool.

Stepping forward, I gripped my toes over the slippery edge. With knees slightly flexed and arms raised, I got ready to dive.

Peering down, I tried to locate the underwater rock. I couldn't see its shadow anywhere.

I stepped back from the edge and turned to Jojo.

"I can't find the rock," I told him.

"You're just chicken, man," he said, sticking his neck out like one.

"We're diving too late, Jojo."

"You're chickenshit, man."

"That guy's accident made us get up here too late."

"Like I said, Pack, you're chickenshit."

"There's no sun on the water, Jojo."

"Chickenshit!"

"Jojo, I can't see the rock!"

"You lose, buddy! You owe me!"

He punched a fist into my chest.

I went down on one knee, lost my balance, and tumbled head-first off the ledge.

As I fell, a gust of wind blew through the kukui trees surrounding the pool. Silver-green leaves fluttered, the last rays of afternoon sun hit the water.

I saw the shadow of the rock.

As I plunged through the dark surface of the water, I twisted my body to one side.

It was ice-cold, blind-black underwater.

I kept my arms extended, trying to protect myself from the rock.

Then I brushed against it, my hands sliding down its slimy side.

I pushed away. I was safe, home free.

Heart pounding, I clawed my way back up to the surface.

Bursting upward into the light, I grinned with relief and waved my arms wildly at the cheering crowd around the pool.

"Way to go, Pack! Way to go!" they said.

Even Kalei stood and clapped.

Treading water, I gulped a mouthful and blew a stream skyward. Now Jojo would owe me five bucks if he didn't follow me down.

"You did it, Packy! You did it!" someone shouted.

Swimming to the side of the pool, I suddenly realized I didn't want Jojo's money. I just wanted to do something better than him.

I climbed out of the water and turned to look up at the ledge.

"No!" I shouted.

Jojo was already in motion, doing a perfect swan dive through the still air.

They brought him out at six that evening.

Shells

They gave Tutu Nui the child on her seventy-fifth birthday.

"She's only six, but she'll be good for you," her grandson said. He reached inside the ancient station wagon, extracted a worn cardboard box, and placed it on the ground next to the girl.

Tutu Nui looked at the slight figure standing in the light morning drizzle, head bowed.

"Whose baby?" The old woman kept her eyes on the child.

"Blackjack's, I guess." Her grandson glanced at the little girl. "He appeared out of nowhere with her. Said

Lani ran off someplace. He can't find her, and he can't keep the kid."

"No good fruit comes from rotten mango trees," Tutu Nui told him. "The child's staying here a few days?"

Her grandson opened his car door before answering. "She has to live here, Tutu Nui. No one else has room for her."

"You mean, no one else wants her." Tutu Nui inspected the girl, dark as her own shadow, staring at the ground. The old woman looked at her grandson. "What happens if I say no?"

"She's hānai, yours to keep." He slid into the driver's seat and closed the door. The engine roared to life, sputtered, then roared again as the car bounced down the lane leading back to the main shoreline road.

Drawing in gaunt cheeks over toothless gums, Tutu Nui stood facing the girl. An incomplete child, she thought. No meat on her, hair growing out in tufts, feet and head too big for her body. Hānai, a child given to someone else to raise.

Tutu Nui moved closer. The child hunched inward, as if trying to make herself smaller. Blinking rapidly to clear the film over her eyes, the elderly woman placed a hand under the youngster's chin and forced the round face upward. The girl flinched when raindrops landed on her eyelids.

"What's your name, child?" Tutu Nui asked.

"Mahina."

Moon. A moon child, thought the old woman.

"But they call me Minnow." Her voice sounded like it lived hunkered down inside the oversized head.

Minnow. An insignificant thing.

"Take your clothes inside." Tutu Nui waved a hand toward the house. The flimsy wooden building, scoured ash-white by blowing sands from the beach fronting the seaside property, stayed moored to the earth by thick cables of cup-of-gold and liliko'i vines. The wild creepers twisted their way up the sides and over the roof of the small structure; an intoxicating stench of rotting fruit and flowers filled the inside rooms.

On the narrow veranda, Tutu Nui turned to watch Minnow enter the house, but the girl hadn't moved. She stood in the misty rain beside her belongings.

"E! Come inside, child." Tutu Nui steadied herself on the porch railing.

Minnow reached down, grasped one side of the cardboard box, and dragged the carton to the bottom of the plank steps. She looked up at Tutu Nui.

"Bring your things inside," the old woman said again. She sank into a waiting rattan chair, angled to catch any breeze that penetrated the grove of coconut palms surrounding the house. Through a gap in the trees, she could see the sandy beach and the ocean beyond, the sea and sky blending together without a horizon.

Tutu Nui looked down at Minnow standing motionless at the foot of the stairs. With a sigh, she closed her eyes, leaving the child to herself.

Picking at the edge of her ragged shorts, Minnow waited until the old woman's mouth went slack and she began to snore, raspy breath vibrating her thin lips. Now the child pushed the heavy box under the porch steps, turned and walked across the sparse lawn that wandered through the palms and ended at the beach. The tough buffalo grass pricked her bare feet. Hot sand burned her soles. She raced to the water's edge and waded in.

Tutu Nui sprawled in her chair all day, opening watery eyes now and then, sightless in slumber. Two large hairpins, holding a coil of hair at the nape of her neck, worked loose. The gray-white strands fell across her shoulders. She slept the sleep of the aged, deep and dreamless.

The sweltering humidity roused Tutu Nui in the late afternoon. She gazed about her. Gradually her mind opened to the events of the day and she remembered the child. Clutching the hem of her faded muʻumuʻu, Tutu Nui stood and went indoors.

The scorching sun hadn't pierced the deep tangle of foliage on the roof. The house remained cool and dim, and empty.

Tutu Nui went outside again and descended the

steep front steps. At the bottom of the stairs, she anchored herself to a rail post and peered under the porch. The child's cardboard box sat in the dirt. Inching forward, Tutu Nui lifted a torn flap and looked inside. The carton contained myriad seashells. Bits of coral and a fish head, the black eye sockets emphasized by the whiteness of bone, lay on top of the collection.

The old woman turned and faced the beach, squinting into the sun. A dark shape crouched in the sand, next to the fishing rack. Solomon's casting net stretched across the rickety frame, thrown there long ago when her husband gave up the old ways of fishing. Unable to catch fish with his net, Solomon tried dynamite, exploding it a foot above the ocean's surface to send a shock wave through the water. The illegal method of fishing cost him his life; he had held a live dynamite stick too long. Tutu Nui felt the gods of the sea had taken their pound of flesh. The old casting net remained draped over the rack under the palms nearest the water. Minnow sat in its shade.

Tutu Nui saw the girl place shells in a pile under the rack, then rise and trot to a mound of rocks that jutted out into the miniature bay. The coral rocks formed a natural breakwater that arced across the opening of the inlet. Receding tides exposed the top of the barrier.

Retreating into the shade of a palm, Tutu Nui sat on a discarded kitchen chair and watched Minnow pick her way along the coral reef. Once the girl stopped and examined something at her feet, then tucked it into her shapeless red tee shirt, held bag-like at her waist.

Resting her eyes from the glaring sun, Tutu Nui slid into a half-sleep, letting the heat of the afternoon cradle her with its warmth.

A cry sliced into her world. Tutu Nui opened her eyes and scanned the reef. On the far side of it, Minnow splashed about in the water. The eddy of incoming waves kept forcing her away from the breakwater as she tried to swim back to it. Tutu Nui knew when her tiny body got close to the reef the backwash would pull her under and the pressure of the waves would pin her against the coral wall.

The old woman struggled to her feet, keeping in sight the spot where Minnow was fighting frantically against the waves. She shuffled to the fishing rack and pulled the casting net down. Stepping out of her lau hala slippers, Tutu Nui dragged the mesh net across the sand to the pile of rocks where the reef began. Lifting the net to a shoulder, she moved out onto the breakwater toward Minnow.

Suddenly the child disappeared.

Tutu Nui stumbled and went down on one knee. Rising slowly under the weight of the net, the old woman staggered forward, the coral cutting into her bare feet.

A flash of red.

Tutu Nui could see Minnow pinned underwater

against the reef's seaward wall. The woman gathered the casting net in her arms. Holding onto a tentacle of it, she threw the bundle into the sea a few feet past the submerged child.

The eddy sucked the net underwater. It brushed against Minnow. The child clawed at it, fighting the current.

With the last of her strength, Tutu Nui pulled in the casting net. A small hand reached up through the mesh; the old woman grabbed it. Minnow emerged from the churning water, choking and coughing.

Tutu Nui and Minnow clung to each other as they worked their way back along the reef. When they reached the shore, the child crawled up the sloping beach and disappeared into the shelter of the palms.

Tutu Nui dropped to her knees and bent forward, supporting her body with her hands. Her head throbbed as blood surged inside it. The swelling exploded into a wave of excruciating pain. She collapsed on the blistering sand and lay still. The harsh rays of the sun caused an earth-spinning dizziness. When she opened her eyes, the glare from the bleached sand blinded her.

"Minnow, help me," she whispered. Hands digging into the soft sand, Tutu Nui closed her eyes as the blackness closed in.

Heat waves rose around her.

•

Shadows of palm fronds danced on the beach while the white moonlight swept across the still water. Tutu Nui lay on her side in the sand, her muʻumuʻu stiff with dried saltwater. An old Hawaiian quilt, a green breadfruit pattern appliquéd on it, had been thrown over her. She shrugged off the heavy coverlet and sat up.

The old woman found a bowl of water beside her. She reached for it greedily, spilling some of the water as she raised it to parched lips, and gulped down the cool liquid. Setting the bowl down in the sand, she saw the shells. Hundreds of seashells of every shape, size, and color encircled her. A ring of incandescence.

Tutu Nui rose to her feet. Dragging the quilt behind her, she started up the slight incline of the beach.

The girl waited in the shadow of the palm trees.

"Mahina," Tutu Nui said.

The child stepped out of the darkness, into the moonlight, and walked beside the old woman toward the lighted house.

Changing Places in Time

She sat high in the tree, eating a ripe mango, letting the yellow juice ooze out the corners of her mouth. It dripped, like soft lemon Jello, onto her bare legs. She waited for Daddy Ray's call.

"Evalani!"

Her stepfather stood by the old Ford next to the house. She could see the bald spot on top of his head; it caught the sun for a moment and glistened.

"Evalani!" Daddy Ray called again, this time leaving the car and striding down the grassy slope. He stopped directly under her and peered up into the mantle of glossy leaves.

"Goddamn it," he said. "Where are you?"

Evalani hunched over and drew in her elbows, holding them tightly against her body, trying to make herself smaller. With the movement, the slimy mango seed slipped from her grasp and fell to her stepfather's feet.

"I know you're up there, Evalani. It's time to go. Now."

Daddy Ray waited for her as she scrambled down, pausing a moment on each lower limb. When she dropped the last few feet to the ground, he grabbed her arm and led her to the car.

"In. And stay there." He pulled open the door and pushed her onto the front seat of the hot, dusty automobile.

As soon as her stepfather walked away, Evalani climbed into the back and wedged her thin body between a pile of cardboard boxes and an open window. She put her feet up on the seat and hugged her knees. Her fingers felt sticky from the mangoes she had been eating all morning; she gave each a quick lick, then sucked off the dried juice.

The kitchen screen door banged. A moment later, Daddy Ray got into the sweltering car with the last suitcase. Without a glance in her direction, he gunned the engine, slammed into gear, and shot down the gravel driveway.

She didn't look back; she didn't live there anymore.

They pulled onto the narrow highway that led into town. The first few miles, the smooth blacktop road ran along the coast, skirting shaggy ironwoods, immovable hau trees, and wind-whipped dunes.

Evalani moved closer to the window and felt the sultry trade wind on her face. When she was small, her mother used to hold her in her arms, in the front seat, and let her stick her head out the window, like a dog sniffing the air.

Now she glanced up at the cracked rearview mirror. Daddy Ray's eyes were framed in it. She immediately hooded her gaze, looking down at her legs. Mahogany color, they jutted from her old blue shorts.

Evalani pushed herself forward to the edge of the seat and thrust her head out the window. She opened her mouth wide and let the hot air rush in; at first, it took her breath away. When she could breathe again, she whispered into the rushing wind, "Mama, can you see me?"

"Get your head inside," Daddy Ray said over his shoulder.

She slumped back against the torn upholstery and leaned to one side until she managed to get a wad of string from her hip pocket. She unraveled the dirty cord and smoothed it out across her knees. Next she undid the top button of her faded shirt and pulled the lapels away from her body. Picking up the string again, she tied it around her neck, letting the long loose end dangle down against her flat chest.

"Mama, can you see me?" The words strangled in her throat.

She used to have a pet chicken. She would talk to it and take it for walks, using the string as a leash. Her mother called the scrawny bird Lovey's Dovey, my little chickadee's chicken. One day, Dovey was gone forever, just like Mama.

She stared at the back of her stepfather's neck. Her eyes glazed over, lost in remembering. Daddy Ray jerked his head around, flashing her an angry look.

"What the hell do you think you're doing with that damn string?"

She sat up straighter and looked out the window. They were on Lahaina Ledge, ten miles of sheer seaside cliffs. As they climbed the first grade, she peered down at the rocks far below. Incoming dark waves beat against them, leaving behind swirling white water. Only a low metal guard rail kept sentry along the narrow, winding road.

Evalani half-stood as they approached Pele's Pass, a treacherous hairpin turn midway through the Ledge. In the distance, she saw the break in the railing.

She glanced at her stepfather, his eyes pinned on the deep curve ahead. She shifted her body and saw his hands gripping the wheel, knuckles white.

They were going too fast, just like Mama.

Evalani grabbed the back of the driver's seat and pulled herself up to a full standing position. At that very moment, unwanted images of Daddy Ray came, flashing in front of her.

Evalani raised her arms and wrapped them around her stepfather's head, putting her hands over his eyes.

"What the hell?" Daddy Ray twisted his head to one side. He tried to pull her hands off his face; they dug in deeper, pressing against his eyeballs.

"Evalani!" he screamed. The tires screeched as he slammed on the brakes. The car skidded and broke through the guard rail.

For a moment in time, Evalani and Daddy Ray were airborne, climbing toward the sun. Then the pull of the earth plummeted them toward the sea.

Falling, falling, the child cried aloud, "Mama, can you see me?"

House of Miseries

He sat on the small decaying pier, legs dangling over the edge, bare feet submerged in warm, murky water. Large scabs covered more of him than his dirty, ragged clothes. The midday island sun beat down on his dark head; no hat or cap would stay anchored to the mass of matted hair. Every few moments, his head twitched to the right, then fell heavily on his chest. He could have been fifty; he was twelve.

Akira, a sun-dark man in faded pants, walked onto the pier that jutted over the mullet pond. In one hand he held a long-poled net. In the other he carried a metal bucket of tiny silvery fish; water slopped over the rim onto his zori.

Stopping behind the boy, he placed the net and the pail on the worn wood and softly spoke the boy's name.

"Kenji."

When he did not respond, Akira slipped his hands beneath the youngster's arms, lifted him up, and set him down again in front of the rusty container.

"Catch the pretty fish," the man said.

Kenji dropped his filthy hands into the bucket and began to whip the clear liquid into a foamy frenzy. When the water splashed over the edge, the boy increased his stirring. The man stood close by, watching the wet circle around the boy expand.

Suddenly, Kenji jerked violently, fell backward, and hit his head on the water-stained decking. No cry of pain left his lips; he lay staring up at the cloudless sky while his arms and legs beat aimlessly.

The man knelt and lifted the boy's head off the rotted planks. With a quick thrust, he smashed a fist against the boy's chin. Then, bracing his legs under him, the man slid his arms under the boy's body, stood up, and walked to the end of the pier.

There Akira lowered the boy into a rowboat. Before he stepped into the small craft, he dumped the bucket of baby mullet into the pond. Untying the rope that tethered the boat to the dock, he climbed into it.

After pushing off from the nearest piling, Akira picked up the oars and slipped them into the brackish water, pulling backward as they broke the surface.

Using one oar in a dipping action, he pointed the rowboat toward an earthen ramp on the other side of the mullet pond. In minutes he beached the boat, jumped overboard into the muddy water, waded to the bow, and pulled the small vessel up onto the sandy soil. Now he reached in and, with a loud grunt, lifted the boy's limp body. Trudging up the incline of the low rock wall enclosing the pond, Akira went down on one knee for a moment as he shifted the boy's weight onto a shoulder.

He walked along the levee, stepping over the tops of several sluice gates that let in fresh water from an adjoining stream. When he came to the corner of the pond, he walked down a trampled grass path that led to a dilapidated building in the distance.

In the clearing surrounding the shack, where bantam chickens pecked at invisible insects and white ducks squatted in shallow indentations in the dirt, he whistled a two-toned signal. Sunao, a woman in an old kimono, appeared immediately on the low-slung front porch. When she saw the man and the boy, she put a hand over her mouth and slowly sank to her knees. She stared, unblinking, and moaned.

"It happened again," Akira said. "On the pier."

Now the woman raised herself, went down the

three rickety steps, and approached the man and his burden.

"Give him to me," she said softly and extended her arms. "Let me have him. Please?"

Without answering her, Akira walked over to the railess porch and placed the boy on the rough planks. The woman, watching from the yard, didn't move. She squinted in the bright sunlight, finally raising an arm and shielding her eyes.

"Leave him alone. Don't touch him," Akira said as he went up the porch steps. He jerked open the sagging screen door and disappeared into the semi-darkness of the dwelling.

The woman waited until the broken door stopped banging back and forth against the crooked frame. She turned around twice, looking at the squawking chickens and preening ducks. Suddenly, she grabbed the nearest bantam and, in the same movement, snapped its neck. With the dead fowl dangling from one hand, she returned to the porch and sat down on the topmost step. She began to pluck the warm mass, pulling feathers from the main body, never looking at her hands. The chicken sprouted dark red pimples.

She stared at the boy lying a short distance away. He had wet himself. It must have just happened because the smell of urine was strong, hanging in the air. The flies in the yard hadn't picked up the scent yet.

When she saw the boy make a slight movement, she

stopped pulling at the scrawny fowl, pushed it off her lap, and crawled the few feet to his side. She sat up, turned the boy over onto his back, and slipped one of her knees under his upper body. Sitting there with his head cradled in her lap, she ran a hand over his tangled hair and kissed his forehead.

The man came out of the house, glanced at the two entwined on the porch, and sat down on the top step, next to the dead chicken. The flies had found it, preferring this warm, exposed body to the urine-covered one.

Akira waved a hand over the bare-skinned fowl lying in the dust of the unswept porch. The flies merely changed altitude to avoid the intruding arm, which soon dropped to the man's side again.

"We can't do this anymore," Akira said.

The woman hugged Kenji closer to her.

"He gets away from you too easily. I can't work in the mullet ponds and watch him."

The woman lowered her head over the boy's face. He did not open his eyes, even when her warm breath touched his face.

"He must go. There is a house in the village that will take him. He will be with others like himself."

Sunao did not speak.

"We can't help him. We can't protect him any-more."

Sunao did not look up.

"He must go," Akira said again. "He must go."

He stood up and walked swiftly out of the yard and down the dirt road. Soon he disappeared into a cane-brake in the distance.

The woman raised her head and looked into the young boy's face. Then she laid her head against his and whispered his name.

"Kenji. Kenji, wake up."

She said this over and over again until the boy roused and opened his eyes.

"Mama. Mama," he said, barely moving his lips.

"I'll go with you, Kenji," the woman said as she stroked his arm. "I'll go with you. You are still my son."

That afternoon, Akira returned to their tin-roofed shack with a short, dark man. His face was deeply pocked. Sunao knew he lived in the place everyone called The House of Miseries and helped the old women there care for those with sick minds and bodies. Now he had come for her son.

Kenji was asleep on a tatami mat on the porch. He had been too heavy for Sunao to carry inside, so she brought his sleeping mat out to him. He curled up on a corner of it, with a thumb in his mouth.

Akira barely glanced at her as he said to the man with him, "This is Sunao, my wife."

The man bowed quickly and said, "I am Yoshi-mura."

Sunao only nodded in return.

Both men approached the sleeping youngster and Akira leaned over him and shook his shoulder. The boy opened his eyes and looked around, dazed.

"Come," said Akira. "Come with me." As he spoke, he reached down and lifted the boy to his feet. Kenji was half-asleep, and his legs would not support his body. He crumpled back onto the mat.

"Get up!" Akira commanded.

Now Kenji struggled to his feet and, hanging onto the two men, stumbled down the porch steps and across the open yard.

Sunao stepped forward and grabbed Akira's arm.

"No! You can't do this," she said.

"Do not try to stop me." Akira pulled his arm away. "We have kept this boy in our house too many years. It is over. This is not his home anymore."

"Please," begged Sunao as she clutched his arm again. "Please!"

Akira pushed her aside and picked up Kenji, once more carrying him over his shoulder like a heavy sack.

The boy did not utter a sound as the men left the yard and headed down the road. A band of swaggering mynah birds made aggressive caws near a wild bamboo clump.

For a long time, Sunao sat where she had fallen. The chickens had gone to roost in the kiawe trees behind the house and the ducks were asleep under the porch. She was huddled there, in the dirt, when Akira returned hours later, the day almost gone.

"Have you lost your mind, like your son?" he asked. "Do you want to live in The House of Miseries, too?"

"I want to live with my son," she mumbled. "I want to live with my son."

Akira did not hear her answer. He was already in the house. He called to her to come in, tired after two trips to town, hungry for his soba noodles.

Sunao rose slowly when she heard Akira call. Instead of entering the house, she went down the old road that led to town. Halfway there, a yellow dog lay on the side of the narrow, dusty road. Its mouth was open and full of flies; the bloating would come later. Sunao didn't cross to the other side as she drew near the dead dog. Nor did she avert her eyes; she saw nothing.

As she hurried along, again and again she wiped the sticky salt from her upper lip and rubbed the back of her hand down the side of her frayed kimono, a flimsy blue wrap tied at the waist with a white cord. She had never been to town in her kimono. The early evening coolness curled under it and made her shiver as she walked.

When she entered the main section of the small plantation town, she untied her sash and slipped out of her kimono, letting it drag behind her, disturbing the thick layer of summer dust. Naked, Sunao paraded through the center of town.

People stopped and stared, but no one said a word to her. Young runners, however, carried the news ahead, announcing her coming. More townspeople came out of their houses and stood in their doorways or on their porches. In silence, they watched her pass.

When she had walked halfway through the town, someone said, "Tell Akira to come quick!" and a messenger was sent to the outlying shack by the mullet ponds.

Finally Sunao left the people behind and traveled a path that disappeared into an overgrown weed field. Now she chose each step carefully and, with an outstretched arm, parted the taller weeds as she made her way.

Suddenly she stopped and cocked her head. She heard the wind in the trees across the field, but nothing else. No one came after her. Not yet.

She went on, slowly, holding her kimono bunched against her bare breasts. It was almost dark now.

Again she stopped, and this time she faced about and leaned into the darkness behind her. As she did so, a figure appeared. The growing shape turned into Akira, dressed for the night air.

Sunao stood quietly and let her husband come toward her, but when he reached her she raised her arms high, threw back her head, and screamed. It was a mournful sound, loud and wailing.

Akira put one arm around her and with the other pressed her head against his body, smothering the noise coming from her gaping mouth. Sunao did not resist; she closed her eyes and collapsed against him.

A voice called in the darkness, across the dark field.

"Where are you?"

Lights hopped through the weeds as more voices called.

"We heard a scream."

"Did you find her?"

"Yes. Yes, I'm over here," Akira called back.

Then he covered Sunao with her dirty kimono and the people helped him carry her across the field and back down the narrow road to the town and her son.

Fighting Cocks

Domingo arrived at the Pau Hana Retirement Home in Lahaina, Maui, in a brand-new lavender low-rider. It belonged to the flashy bachelors of the plantation workers' camp; as is the custom, they had banded together and invested in a club car.

After unloading Domingo's many string-tied parcels and burlap bundles, the young men got back into the shiny automobile, waved goodbye, and departed with collective dignity.

"Mabuhay!" Domingo said, and grinned at the crowd of elderly people standing in the common area facing their small bungalows. The occupants of all twenty-eight cottages had gathered to watch the retired

97

pineapple picker's arrival. Some of the women smiled shyly at the never-married Filipino; three men helped him carry his belongings to his assigned one-room bungalow. They soon found out that one of the burlap bags held a big tethered bird.

The day after Domingo's arrival, the Sakamotos saw him walk briskly down Nahaku Road to the local market. While he was gone, they peered curiously through his screen door and saw a fine-looking rooster strutting around his living room. When the other residents heard this news, they waited anxiously for a dawn crowing. None came.

"It's a fighting cock," old Mr. Macadangdang told everyone who mentioned the fowl. "Fighting cocks don't crow. Their vocal chords have been cut so the authorities won't hear them."

Mr. Macadangdang had lived at the retirement settlement for over fifteen years; he had worked on a sugar plantation until he was too old to cut cane. When his wife's death ended their childless marriage, he moved to Pau Hana. This place of "no work" was acceptable to him because he was allowed to grow flowers around his bungalow. Over the years, through selective cross-pollinating and tireless attention, he had succeeded in raising prize-winning blooms.

One afternoon, Mr. Macadangdang sat in front of a checkerboard balanced on an upturned pineapple crate, hoping someone would challenge him to a game.

Seldom did anyone stop to play; Mr. Macadangdang always won.

"Mabuhay," said Domingo. He placed a paper bag of groceries on the ground and squatted down on the empty packing box facing Mr. Macadangdang. "I can play?" he asked.

In less than half an hour, the game was over. Domingo won. The first Pau Hana resident to beat Mr. Macadangdang.

A silent crowd had formed around the two players, and when Domingo said, "Play again?" they all nodded. This time the game lasted longer, but the outcome was the same. Domingo won.

When Domingo asked Mr. Macadangdang if he wanted to try once more to beat him, the older man rose slowly and, without a parting word, retreated to his bungalow. No one saw him for three days.

On the fourth day, the manager of the old folks home appeared at Domingo's bungalow. Banging on the screen door, the man yelled into the cool darkness within.

"Domingo? Do you have a fighting cock in there? Domingo, answer me!"

Wearing his customary faded shorts and rubber thongs, Domingo came to the door, opened it narrowly, and slipped outside. Shifting from one foot to the other, he told the manager, "I no have fighting cock. I have dumb chicken."

"No pets," the manager said.

"Chicken no pet. Just living here."

"No animals of any kind allowed at Pau Hana, Domingo. You know that. Get rid of that damn rooster or suffer the consequences."

"Suffer the consequences? What that mean?"

"Keep the cock, lose your place here. I'll check on you tomorrow, Domingo." The manager walked directly to his car, got in, and drove away.

Domingo stood in front of his bungalow and yelled at all the screen doors facing him.

"Who told? Who told da kine boss man? My rooster is retired, just like me. Who told on him?"

The screen doors remained silent.

Domingo turned and squinted at Mr. Macadang-dang's bungalow. He stared at it for a long time before going indoors. Minutes later, his neighbors saw him come out of his cottage with a burlap bag. He wore a shirt and shoes so everyone knew he was going into town.

Several hours later, Domingo returned empty-handed to Pau Hana. He passed several residents collecting ripe fruit from the mango trees that fringed the settlement. No greeting or helping hands from Domingo this time. He went straight to his bungalow. No one heard or saw him until the next morning.

At 6 A.M., Domingo came out of his bungalow and crossed the grassy patch to Mr. Macadangdang's bungalow. He stood squarely before the old man's prize flowers. Unzipping his khaki shorts, he fumbled for a moment. Then, with one arm raised in a fist salute and shouting "Mabuhay!," he urinated on the lush blooms.

The bungalow's screen door burst open and Mr. Macadangdang, bolo knife in hand, confronted Domingo. Both men stood frozen for an instant. Then Mr. Macadangdang, slicing the air with his two-foot cane cutter, chased Domingo across the yard.

Domingo darted agilely back and forth, avoiding the razor-sharp weapon. Suddenly he raced for the safety of his own bungalow, slammed the screen door, and locked the wooden one behind him.

Mr. Macadangdang stood on Domingo's small slab porch, swinging his giant knife and shouting every known combination of pidgin-English swear words. He was only a pair of pants removed from the jungle. Finally he marched back to his garden and dropped to his knees before his beloved flowers. He never got up.

Everyone said Mr. Macadangdang's heart killed him. Domingo knew better.

Taming Unseen Dragons

Ama picked up her sharpest knife, slit open the blow-fish, and removed the poisonous liver and ovaries lodged within. She placed the deadly, blood-red lumps beside the wooden chopping board. Removing the skin, bones, and dark portions from the fish, she cut the white meat diagonally into thin strips. Then, arranging them on a platter, she slipped the sashimi slices into an old refrigerator humming in a corner of the small kitchen.

"Ama," Toki called from the bedroom. Her husband's weak voice slid through the stillness of their bungalow.

Placing the knife in a pan of water in the sink, Ama

wiped her hands on her apron and stared out the kitchen window.

The screen filtered the shimmering mist of heat that lay over Kalaupapa. The leper colony, nestled between sheer cliffs and the ocean, seemed to be holding its breath, waiting for a breeze to move the heavy humid air out to sea.

Toki called again.

Ama pulled off her damp apron and padded across the clean-swept linoleum into the adjoining bedroom. Their sleeping room, full of shadows cast by the drawn reed blinds, couldn't hide the disfigurements of the man lying on the bed.

Kneeling beside Toki, Ama picked up her husband's claw-like hand and stroked it.

"Would you like something to eat?"

At the sound of her voice, Toki turned his head toward her, blinking at the ceiling. "Stay with me, Ama, stay with me." She would stay. She had chosen lifetime exile at the leper settlement rather than suffer separation.

Ama got off her knees and sat down beside her husband. "Toki, I want you to eat. I've fixed sashimi."

"Look at me, Ama." He put his free hand over hers. "What do I look like now?"

Ama brushed the dark hair off his forehead and laid her cheek against his. She felt the roughness of his unshaven skin.

"Ah, Toki," she said, looking at his ulcerated face.

"You're handsome to me." She squeezed his hand and the disfigured face before her tried to smile. Lesions had eaten away her husband's nose, leaving a gaping hole that drained pus into his mouth cavity. As she spoke, he groped for the rag beside him on the bed and wiped the yellowish-green matter away.

She remembered his kisses: when he returned home from fishing, they tasted of the sea. When he brought home a shirtful of guavas, they were wet and sweet, like the fruit he loved.

Now Ama slipped her hand from his grasp. Turning him onto his side, she folded back the clean white sheet, exposing his naked body. The leprosy had thickened his skin. Raised nodules covered his back, like knotted rope under his discolored skin. She kneaded the remaining folds of loose flesh around his waist. The senses in every part of her body were awakened as she remembered Toki before the disease took hold.

Before they came to live in this isolated place, he loved to fight invisible dragons. When they went to the beach, he would begin to move in a circle, eyes dilated, nostrils flared. Brandishing a sugarcane-stalk javelin or a driftwood club, he would thrust himself forward, again and again, kicking up sand and snorting loudly. The muscles in his broad back rippled in sharp relief. Holding his arms high and wide, he would resume the slow circling, growling deep in his throat. When she laughed, he would pounce upon her, lay her gently down on the sand, and hold her tight. Later, he would take her home and make love to her until the moon rose over a shoulder of the mountain behind their old house.

Now she scanned his near-lifeless body. Wherever her eyes moved, her lips followed.

At her touch, Toki groaned.

Ama turned her husband onto his back again, pulled the sheet over his nakedness, and fled before the tears began. On her way to the kitchen, she heard Toki call out. It sounded like a child's cry.

Ama would not consent to having a baby. Doctors at the clinic discouraged children. Although the disease was not highly contagious, they felt leprosy threatened newborns. All babies born to lepers were taken away. She told Toki they had lost enough.

In the kitchen, Ama placed a pan of water on a burner and, striking a kitchen match, lighted their ancient gas stove. When the water came to a boil, she shut off the stove and placed an opened bottle of sake in the pan. Slumping into a chair, she closed her eyes and listened to the roaring within.

Toki's cries roused her.

Retrieving the platter of sliced fish, Ama took the sashimi and warm sake into the bedroom.

"Toki, you must eat," she said.

"Help me!" Her husband's words gurgled from deep inside his chest. His body dripped with a putrid-smelling sweat.

Placing the sashimi and sake bottle on a table next to the bed, Ama hurried back to the kitchen for the forgotten chopsticks.

A sharp cry pierced the silence.

Ama stopped in front of the chopping block. She stared at the remains of the blowfish, unseeing.

"Ama!" Toki's shrill cry ripped open the night.

She snatched up a pair of chopsticks and the blowfish ovaries. The sacs of poison felt warm in the palm of her hand.

At Toki's bedside, she dropped the fish ovaries onto the platter and, without hesitating, picked up one of them with the chopsticks. Using her free hand, Ama raised her husband's head.

"Eat this, Toki. Now!"

Crying out for her, Toki opened his mouth. Ama pushed the tiny sac inside it. Dropping the chopsticks, she clamped his mouth shut. Struggling weakly, Toki swallowed.

Ama picked up the chopsticks once more.

Her pain came with terrifying speed, and the sound of her grief filled the empty hills and sky, taming the unseen dragons.